GRANDMA'S BILL

MARTIN WADDELL

Illustrated by
JANE JOHNSON

MACDONALD YOUNG BOOKS

For Darrell – J.J.

For Sally Doran – M.W.

First published in Great Britain in 1990 by
Simon & Schuster Young Books

Reprinted in 1992 and 1994

Reprinted in 1997, 1998 and 1999 (twice) by
Macdonald Young Books
an imprint of Wayland Publishers Ltd
61 Western Road
Hove
East Sussex
BN3 1JD

Printed and bound in Belgium by Proost International Book Production

British Library Cataloguing in Publication Data
Waddell, Martin
Grandma's Bill
I. Title II. Johnson, Jane
823'.914 [J]

ISBN 0 7500 0307 3

Every Thursday Bill went to tea with his Granny.

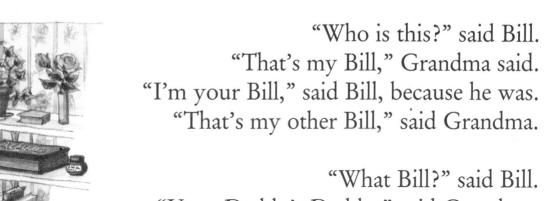

"Who is this?" said Bill.
"That's my Bill," Grandma said.
"I'm your Bill," said Bill, because he was.
"That's my other Bill," said Grandma.

"What Bill?" said Bill.
"Your Daddy's Daddy," said Grandma.
"I didn't know Daddy had a Daddy," said Bill.
"Well he had," said Grandma.

"Look, here's my big book of photographs. That's Bill,"
  Grandma said.
"That's a baby!" said Bill.

"He was a baby, to begin with," said Grandma.
"That's his Mummy and Daddy."
"Don't they look funny? said Bill.

"That's Bill again," Grandma said.
"He's not a baby any more," said Bill.
"He's a big boy like you," said Grandma.
"I'm a bit bigger," said Bill.

"Look at him now!" said Grandma.
"He's got funny knees!" said Bill.
"He wore shorts," said Grandma.
"I've got trousers," said Bill, and he showed her.
"So you have!" said Grandma.

"He's grown up in this picture,"
 said Grandma.
"Is that him?" said Bill.
"That's Bill," said Grandma.
"Guess who that is!"

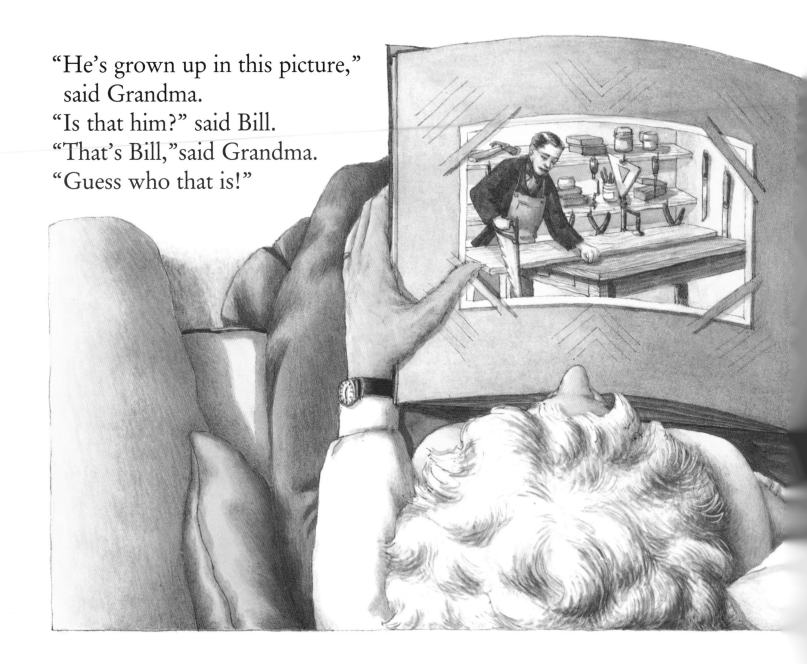

"Who is it?" said Bill.
"Me!" said Grandma.
"No it's not," said Bill.
"You're all wrinkles!"

"That's us getting married," said Grandma.
"Where's your wrinkles?" said Bill.
"I had no wrinkles then," said Grandma.
"You don't look right without wrinkles!"
  said Bill.

"That's Bill in the army,"said Grandma.
"Who is?" said Bill.
"That soldier is," said Grandma.
"He fought in the war."
"Why?" said Bill.
"There was a big war," Grandma said.
"Lots of people fought in it."

"Guess who this one is?" said Grandma.
"Who is it?" said Bill.
"That's your Daddy! That's him with Bill
on the beach when he was a baby.
Your Daddy was my baby," Grandma said.

"Who's that?" said Bill.
"That's your Daddy bigger," said Grandma. "And Bill."

"Why's Bill got a stick?" said Bill.
"He got hurt in the war," said Grandma.

"My Daddy's not in this one," said Bill.
"Yes he is!" said Grandma. "That's him!"
"Where's Bill?" said Bill.

"Bill was working that day," said Grandma.
"Look at your hat!" said Bill. "Have you still got it?"

"That's your Daddy going to school," said Grandma.
"And that's Bill!" said Bill.
"Right!" said Grandma.

"That's your Daddy in his first job," said Grandma.
"Who's that?" said Bill.
"You know who that is!" said Grandma.
"No I don't," said Bill.

"That's your Mummy," said Grandma.

"They look funny getting married," said Bill.
"People do," said Grandma.
"Is that you in the hat?" said Bill.
"Yes," said Grandma.
"Why's Bill got that funny chair?" said Bill.
"His legs didn't work properly," said Grandma.

"That's OUR HOUSE!" shouted Bill.
"And me and your Mummy and Bill," said Grandma.

"Where's my Daddy?"
"I think he slept in!" said Grandma.

"Where's *me*?" said Bill.
"You come in soon," said Grandma.

"There's me!" said Bill.
"Yes," said Grandma.

"Where's Bill?" said Bill.
"Bill wasn't there any more," said Grandma.

"Did he die?" said Bill.
"Yes," said Grandma.

"I bet my Daddy was sad," said Bill.
"Everybody was," said Grandma.
"It's all right, though, isn't it?" said Bill.
"Of course it is," said Grandma.

"You've still got a Bill," said Bill.
"I've still got two Bills," said Grandma.
"Where's the other one?" said Bill.
"In my book," said Grandma.
And she closed the book,
and put it back on the shelf.